Congo, seen from the heavens

Book Layout and Design by Alice Lee and Cass Lintz
Copy Edited by Susan Calvillo

Cover Art by Cianga
Courtesy of the artist

Copyright © 2023 Cianga
ISBN: 979-8-9892864-0-9

Cataloging-in-publication data is available from the Library of Congress

This book has been made possible, in part, by a grant from the Zellerbach Family Foundation.

Printed in the United States of America

Foglifter Press
San Francisco, California
www.foglifterpress.com

congo, seen from the heavens

Cianga

kuibidija mpuku chomba,
ni akudila matala

●

●

if you feed a rat your cassava,
it will grow up to eat your field

table of contents

etymology of names...4

hemo/phobia...6

the anger of man...7

the monolith: a psalm...8

apple...12

portrait of Lubumbashi, DRC...13

self-portrait as asylee...14

justification I (golden shovel)...15

the good soil we own(ed)...16

new gen african...18

Congo, seen from the heavens...19

portrait of a black dancer...20

in defense of french...22

linguistics, broken...23

powerful, beyond measure...24

okra...26

running to[ward]...27

erasure of the Congolese national anthem...28

acknowledgements...29

etymology of names

I.

before democracy, there was
a river, single stream. before
deer tongues. before nomad
fish frenzied. before the land   split
coltan lesions and *wept*. before
the river sought its name and
found it, bleeding, not unlike
a mangosteen: black and red
yet white. before all swallows
learned to yawn their beaks
along water too pacific to fight.
the river, suffered the fate all
bodies of liquid fear: being
classed and *named* and *used*.

II.

stubbornness is a Congolese
mother. sun-ironed skin. *liputa*
securing her young death-grip
across her heart as she bargains
a street vendor bankrupt. loud
eyes trained on all things *fufu*
in potential. her weary talons
grip forcefully enough to hold
a splitting world. collapsing sun.
decaying knees. she unravels her
form: *Zaire*. a gluttonous Congo.
a country of oblique heads. a belly
everyone has robbed at least once.

III.

my name is after God:
a warning, sharper than
the first footfalls of men
who vowed their God,

concealed between hilt
and blade, was *singing
over them*. their pockets
of psalms faded beneath
the equator's callous sun.
just as those men chose
a pet name for a country,
my mother chose a name
that daggers my tongue.
gills my arms. webs my feet.
that among all the binding
names Zaire fights against   i may
breathe and *swim* and *hunt*.

hemo/phobia

all this *blood*
must have escaped

someone alive.
nothing long dead bleeds.

this trail must have begun
a trespass, not unlike Cain

and his bloody offering no
heaven drunk. this blood—

unlike the chemicals
that made the frogs gay—

armed the tadpoles with swords
against the ebola of alarmists.

fearful things. so safe they invent
monsters that echo their visage.

all this *fear*
must have begun

when Mandela offered his fists
to the newborn liberty.

when a young Congo watched,
its own palms forced to dissolve.

when this land forgives
as one would welcome death,

no corpse alives themselves home.
then all our blood,

vengeful platelets clotting graves—
where does it go?

the anger of man

when skin shreds co-pay letters, my teeth
break down my fists. this diaspora.

makes a superhero of my tongue. woe is
my mother. video chats cost bloody cobalt.

i spit a new world when she calls.
i name the ocean between us a child,

capricious; we must learn to discipline
our rage. no one says

i'm so angry i could kiss you.

but i am.
so angry

it's melancholic. to bandage a tongue;
sharpen a feather. as one would a machete.

forget a blade can be windborn. believe
each call is a fight. and all we have left.

the monolith: a psalm

the following music notation is used to note instruction for a Ngoma (Congolese drum) musician:

        ● - **bass**
        ○ - **mid tone**
        ° - **high tone**
        x - **rest**
        — - **finger taps, high tone**
        ♦... - **high tone cadenza, i.e., go free**

february 17, 2021:
    a monolith appeared in Kinshasa.
    silver metal. reflective. tall. as if it could reach God.

°°°°○○○●(x3)
    want is a terrifying verb. we only knew *need*.

○   ○   ○   ○
clawed grip. dagger nails. slow crawl. 'cross crimson soil.

○●   ●
there's a rhythm to survival.

°°°°○○○●   ○   ○   ○   ○   ♦...○
tempo in the *snap* back *growl* tongue. *bang* head *swing* airborne *slam* soil.

●
halt.

°°°°○○○●
the monolith asked us a cruel song. *burn or pray.*

{ ∘∘∘∘○○○●   ∘∘∘∘○○○●   ∘∘∘∘∘∘∘∘
despair. or fold. and yell. weak grip. yell and yell.   *my lord.*

{ ∘∘∘∘○○○●
the voice box is so well-protected.   it dies last.

{ ———
burn or pray. 15 million spirits. not well-versed in arson.   for those.

{ —————————————————○————————————————————
15 million.

{ —●————————————————————————————●
Zaire became a battleground. of prayers.

{ ∘∘∘∘∘∘∘∘∘∘∘∘∘∘∘∘∘●○○○○○○○○○○○○●
to flesh. and teeth. and uniforms.   *lord.*

{ x
to pray to the sole of a shoe.

{ ——
to sing while your country is ablaze.   *my lord.*

{   ●   ● ∘∘∘∘○○○●
the voice box is so well-protected.   it outlives the spirit.

{ x
how else. would he. my brother.

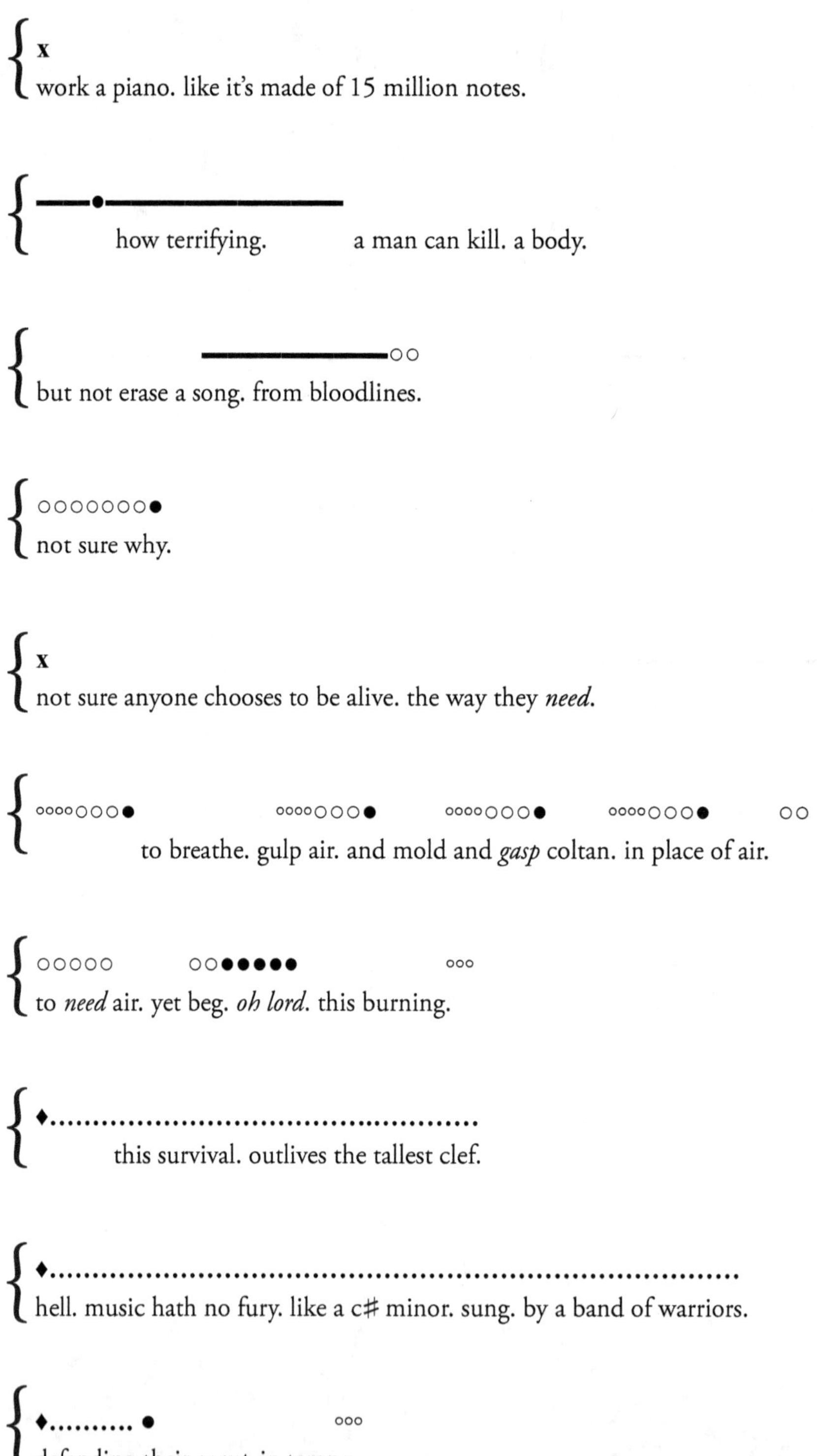

{ x
work a piano. like it's made of 15 million notes.

{
        how terrifying.   a man can kill. a body.

{
but not erase a song. from bloodlines.

{
not sure why.

{ x
not sure anyone chooses to be alive. the way they *need*.

{
            to breathe. gulp air. and mold and *gasp* coltan. in place of air.

{
to *need* air. yet beg. *oh lord*. this burning.

{
        this survival. outlives the tallest clef.

{
hell. music hath no fury. like a c# minor. sung. by a band of warriors.

{
defending their *want*. in tempo.

surely. this desire. unsheathes a machete.

to want. a home.

unbloodied. unbodied. i want.

and *want*. dagger nails. crawl taut.

i burned the monolith.

and its maker.

and spit.

a choir.

apple

It hovered over us, about two weeks. Bulbous head in suspended motion.
We watched it Eve, at weddings, over fufu. At sunrise, we gathered

our young, our printless fingers, our bowed bones, just to look at it. We watched it
become sky. One day, a brick fell on us. Someone declared it holy. Another hell.

Someone else added their own brick to it. *I'm making history.* They proclaimed. We built.
Under the new sky, our rivers dried. We ran out of water to cement the damn bricks.

We built the rest with our blood; the color of something too tired to be red.
Our bravest maggot swam to the top. We reached the sky. Some of us

grew tired. Stuck to the congealed tower and became part of it.
Some of us stayed and drank each other in search of water.

We prayed. It hovered. The poor licked at its edges. We forgot the original
color of rain. We heard yells from those now too far up to ever fall. Their voices,

dead in air, hailed on us. *What a view.* Guffaws. *You could have made here too
if you weren't so weak.* For a week, their yells became our silence.

Beneath. Distant disdain. Their voices distorted with time. Their words ate themselves back up
and retched a dissonant apocalypse. Laughter. All night, that final night, there was laughter.

Could hear their bellies. Expelling so much air. Laughter so shrill and demanding
when we closed our eyes, to the blackness before us, the laughter

could have been
crying.

portrait of Lubumbashi, DRC

feces soil a sad attempt of a sidewalk
●

a missionary brings Jesus on a coltan-rich phone
●

everyone's broke, but no one's poor enough to die
●

a rat boards a rocket that erupts, in the name of science
●

a cardboard box can sing, in the right hands
●

there's too much rain for anything to be permanent
●

the sun is Lubumbashi's last defensive architect
●

cities don't cry when it rains, they cry through the blood of children

[ask why all this foreign aid can't fix the smile off a skull.
ask why the most violent killer in DRC is a child]

all Congolese got beef with some white man
●

i'm no different
●

i'm not really mad, i'm just broke
●

my skin still shrinks when i see a dog fed a child's survival
●

in a city this big, family is whoever remembers you smiling
●

a memory is dangerous when left in a cardboard box
●

a cardboard box is a machete that hasn't grown up yet
●

a city of cardboard boxes is a graveyard

self-portrait as asylee

if a city is its people
& the people are always leaving,
was it ever a home to anyone?

Lubumbashi burned,
but i had a painting due the next day
so the city never wailed.

Lubumbashi burned,
but a new iPhone was due to be released
so the children's funerals were rescheduled.

i want to ask maman
what to do when i see my skin melt off
whenever i hold a battery made of cobalt

i want to ask maman
what good is calling a city a home
if it doesn't know how to love a people alive.

Lubumbashi asks
me, voice aged with decay:
how do you love a people always leaving?

Lubumbashi asks
me, prodigal: *how do you love a people long gone?*
we don't belong here anymore.

justification I (golden shovel):

after Franny Choi and Lembit Beecher

"i had to" laughs the
woman. nervous. "had to." her world

now a music box. mechanical. like Papa. keeps
rewinding his breath; prefers a ghost to an ending.

no refugee outlives their ghosts. the world is a phoenix and
papa is a relic. fit for Louvre and circus in those good pants that kiss the

land. this soil. survived Papa's apocalypse. makes me chimera. makes the world
owned. makes the woman viral. makes Papa a family of stomachs. while the war goes

on.

the good soil we own(ed)

when i move to kill The Man,
He kneels. palms to gravity.
like he belongs to *this* good earth.

daring to cry.
wail.

He lost His shop to arson by locals.
says He can't leave His Son, His Daughter.
       (*my mom* had *a son, a daughter*)

The Man
isn't here colonially.
not to steal & kill.

just rent and buy till
Kinshasa doesn't smell like me. till
the soil becomes our roof.

The Man says He isn't history and
       (*show me your hands*)

He
is a brown

maybe
two shades lighter than mine.

man

says he's a bottom feeder—
just wants a place to work
to feed his son, his daughter

&

I release my grip,
unearth My limbs.
unloving,
unhating,

just —

that seat he has,
bloodied and all,

that seat
used to be Mine.

new gen african

growing pains is
telling my African father *i want snake bites*.

his eyes widen and foam over
our rabid lineage slamming itself hurt over

piercing metal. his fatherhood
an exercise in ambivalence. to watch

a child become a name you did not
give them. to muffle an ancestor

in the name of love. to watch your creation
shed parts of you while blooming.

get them, he says.
won't look me in the eyes.

Congo, seen from the heavens

for Kavira

[the first Congolese to board a space shuttle is a rat]

i unfold
saliva teeth

gnaw at their flag's skin
floss with the fat

i swelter
rabies, love

homeland's got no food
yet, i fly

i devour
the sky

from the troposphere,
every human is a rodent

i rat
pray

for my freedom warriors
more bone than muscle

i ascend,
poverty's defiance

already, love,
i split the sun.

portrait of a black dancer

after D'mani Thomas

walks slow.   stalks the battlefield
foot's a joke gravity's in   on
takes the wind for spin
kind of body any block would miss

say -
*"You ever witness a crowd of people   break
into cha cha slide
          at a First Friday Block Party"*

sounds like -

this town's more black than rhythm   *more*
moonlit flicker jazz charts fingering stars

say -
*"You ever remember?
          how many family members
          can't afford to live here anymore?"*

sounds like -

we   had the funeral over Instagram Story
we   dance shadows on sidewalk oceans
we

last line figured bass brass belly *flop*
onto a pothole made of 19th & Broadway *Lubumbashi* blues

fight   till the walls remember to scream
fight   with all the grace of a human body

on death row   laugh all sharp snap teeth
dance   like breathing is optional
dance   tall chin sky-bound spiral elbows into *woah*

every block rebirths its boombox chorale
every street lamp spotlights you regal
westlake warrior, you make going home a dance

in defense of french

●   *there is*
no french word for <u>i miss you</u>

instead *tu me manque* means
you are missing from me
          [*i.e., you first taste about absence on a colonizer's tongue*]

no french word for <u>longing</u>, either
nothing for how the absence of *Zaire*
desaturates my walk

french word for body, *corps,*
swims back into English as <u>corpse or cadaver</u>
          [*note how the colonizer's tongue turned the body into its absence with the erasure of a word*]

~~i am longing for a language i've never learned but~~
          [*REMEMBER! there is no french word for longing!*]

●   *someone*
asks when i will let this tongue go

but in defense of having a language with which to call home
i answer *ma mère me manque*
          [*i.e., my mother is missing from me*]

●   *listening,*
carefully,

i allow myself a tiny grace
that every spoken sound can bring me home

anything can be a langue if
there is someone listening

linguistics, broken[1]

the Principle of Less Effort states:
we choose the easiest paths.

as applied to linguistics:
we choose the smallest words.

like a story that grows with history
ferments to a pleasant tang (*ngai*)

when characters are plucked from the air
pressed into a notebook, i (*ngai*) curse the tongue

for a page that trembles as loud as Kaku's prayers
for a hero, written, that isn't stripped of their endlessness

ngai and i hold a funeral for everything
too difficult to exist for very long.

---

[1] *ngai* is a Lingala word that can mean *I* or *sour* or a *vegetable*.

powerful, beyond measure

i let the spider live
on the ceiling
above my bed

a week. it disappeared.
we all do.

my deepest fear?

to learn my limits
by name.

that spider –
another must have taught it to web.
must have.

i can hardly escape my bed
yet my blood knows:
i am my ancestor's best outcome.

therefore, i am ancestor
to those who must hear:

history doesn't repeat,
but unravels out of itself.

i'm stealing a lullaby
from Leopold
for our bellied joy.

we, resilient and fragile –

grains that were plucked and dried
and kneaded alive again.

beloved, we must call our limits
by name.

then,
defy them

okra

before my body warped solid, i was a fire
beneath my mother's chipped blade.

gentle callus,
slight scrape 'round charred pan.

i've known you,
from my mother's blood.

known you to deserve *cayenne* and *suya*;
a plate well-loved into aging;

slow simmer;
gentle steam to full sweetness.

before a weblog, photograph,
wistful saliva mouth dissects you for profit.

remember, love:

before my body warped solid, i was a fire
beneath my mother's chipped *blade*.

running to[ward]

                                        [forgiving]

in my every poem
I
frag/ment
pain/full
break/age
so/raw

whatever spills from my pot is for the little ones

                                        [you]

are, therefore I am
joy/us
all/live
heal/thy
some/times
up/praise
my hood
point/sis
purr/fact
star/kin

                                        [all]

ants in my kitchen strut like they've got something to say

my apologies, F/father
for forgetting the purpose of my teeth

erasure of the Congolese national anthem

arise, Congolese,

united by *fate, united in* the struggle for *independence,*
let us hold up our *heads, so long bowed,*
and now, for good, let us keep moving boldly ahead, in peace.

oh, ardent people, by hard work we shall *build,*
in peace, a country *more* beautiful *than before.*
countrymen, sing the sacred *hymn of your solidarity,*
proudly *salute the* golden *emblem of your sovereignty, Congo.*

blessed *gift (Congo) of our forefathers (***Congo***),*
oh beloved *(Congo)* country,
we shall people your soil and ensure your greatness. (30 june) oh
gentle sun *(30 june) of 30 june,*
(holy day) be *witness (holy day) of the* immortal *oath of freedom*
that we pass on to our children

forever.

acknowledgements

Umuntu ngumuntu ngabantu

●

A person is a person because of other people

and I am

because in fifth grade, that bike missed me. Because Tongo wrote a repeating poem and I've yet to end. Because of the Brooklyn Poet's fellowship, where I wrote the title poem. Because of Rose who got a tattoo that makes me feel like I've got something to say. Because of Mr. Klein, who came to my first slam (spoiler: I lost). Because of Gabe, who held a space so warm, I came back the next year (spoiler: I won). Because of all who taught me something beautiful about writing: Natasha, Isa, Arati, Janae, Terisa, Laurel, Kiki, Summer, Ama, Neena, closegood, Mel, Maya, Tamia, Isabella, Azariah, Menat, Ms. Harris, and many more who I've failed to mention but are one phone call away.

Because earlier versions of these poems have lived in:
> *EcoTheo Review*: "okra," "beyond measure," "Congo, seen from the heavens"
> *Rappahannock Review*: "the monolith: a psalm"
> *UC Berkeley ARC's Emerge/ncy*: "portrait of a black dancer," "portrait of
> Lubumbashi," "erasure of the Congolese national anthem."

Because everyone at Foglifter Press has re-colored the definition of support and community love. On community: how would this collection have come without: D'mani, who was with me for every celebration and rejection, Albert, Jessie, and Jessica who've seen me through all my cringe eras; Karina, Jayla, and Teresa who have loved gently, yet unyielding. Lara, dear duo. Shivani, blood of my blood. Bay Poets Unite, EcoTheo, Cave Canem, 3crosses, A2F, Rose Fam, Atlantic Center for the Arts, UC Berkeley ARC. I disappear at least once a year and without them, I would never return.

Lastly: many thanks to my family—my precious treasure. Parfait who loves with open palms, Patrick who carries the world but finds time to enjoy a good anime, Grego who taught me my first art. To my parents who knew when to run and when to stay. To God, who I imagine, was the first to see Congo, from the heavens.

This collection is for and because of you all. You turn my wandering life into a journey. Thank you. Thank you. Thank you.

Rooted in the San Francisco Bay Area, Foglifter Press is a platform for LGBTQ+ writers that supports and uplifts powerful, intersectional, and transgressive queer and trans writing through publication and public readings to build and enrich our communities as well as the greater literary arts.
www.foglifterpress.com